BRANDON ARIAS

SCARS

1

Kana

CONTENTS

CHAPTER 1

I'M REALLY SORRY, KIDDO.
WE JUST CAN'T AFFORD TO PAY FOR PRIVATE LESSONS ANYMORE.
YOU'LL HAVE TO GO BACK TO HIGH SCHOOL.
I'M SCARED...

BLA
BLA
BLA
BLA
BLA
BLA
BLA
BLA

BREATHE...
IT'S GOING TO BE FINE.
DING DONG DANG DONG

HA HA HA
BLA BLA BLA
QUIET DOWN, CLASS!
TODAY, WE WELCOME A NEW STUDENT.
KYONOSUKE, PLEASE COME UP AND INTRODUCE YOURSELF.
OH...
O-OK...

HI, MY NAME IS KYONOSUKE. I'M 15, AND...UM... I HOPE WE CAN BE FRIENDS.
BLA BLA BLA BLA BLA BLA BLA BLA BLA BLA BLA BLA BLA BLA BLA BLA BLA BLA

BLA
BLA
BLA
BLA
BLA
BLA
BLA
BLA

BAM!
OW!
MY BAD. SORRY, DUDE...
I-IT'S OK, I'M FINE.
HA HA HA HA HA
SCORE! I TOTALLY SMASHED HIS FACE IN WITH MY AWESOME SHOT! HA HA HA!
HA

HA HA
HA HA

HA HA HA!
SORRY, I WAS JUST KIDDING AROUND.
ARE YOU OK?
Y-YEAH... I'M FINE, HA HA!
GOOD! LATER, ZOMBIE HEAD.
HA HA

HA HA HA!
...
HA...
HA HA!...
PHEW...

YO! WHAT'S UP, FRANKENSTEIN?
WHAT ARE YOU EATING?
CAN I HAVE SOME? I FORGOT MY LUNCH AT HOME.

THANKS, FRANK!
UH... OK, SURE.
MY NAME IS...
HEY, YOU GOT ANY CASH ON YOU?
LATER, FRANK.

WHATEVER YOU HAVE IS FINE.
HAND IT OVER!
COME ON...
UM... I...NO.

COME ON, FRANK. I REALLY NEED IT, DUDE.
HELP ME OUT, MAN! WHATEVER YOU HAVE IS FINE.
N-NO. WHY SHOULD I GIVE YOU MY MONEY?

WHAT DID YOU SAY?
NO CASH FOR YOU.
NOW LISTEN UP, YOU FREAK.
AAAAHH!!!
EITHER DO AS I SAY, OR I BEAT THE CRAP OUT OF YOU!
AAH, SO- SORRY.
FRSHH

YOU FORGOT TO SAY "SIR"! "I'M SORRY, *SIR!*"
S-SIR!
I'M SORRY, SIR! I'M SORRY!
YANK
YANK

THAT'S BETTER. NOW HAND OVER THE DOUGH.
OK. H-HERE.
NOW PLEASE JUST LET ME GO.
EXCELLENT.
BUT HERE'S A TIP FOR NEXT TIME: DON'T ARGUE, JUST OBEY.

HUUURK
PHHH
AGH
BLA BLA BLA

DING DONG DANG DONG
SEE YOU LATER.
OK, GREAT.
MY PLACE?

CHACK
HI, SWEETIE. HOW DID IT GO?

IT WENT GREAT.
I'M GLAD TO HEAR IT, HONEY. I WAS SO WORRIED.

KYONOSUKE, IT'S TIME TO GET UP...
TOC TOC TOC
I NEED TO GET GOING, KIDDO.
I'M UP...

ALL RIGHT, THAT'S IT FOR TODAY.
CLASS DISMISSED.
YES? KYONOSUKE?
IS THERE A PROBLEM?

UM, NO...
I WAS JUST THINKING ABOUT STUFF...

!
PAF!
SORRY, DON'T MIND ME...
TAP! TAP! TAP!

UM, YEAH...
FRANK, ARE YOU ALL RIGHT?
OH...
YOUR... YOUR ELBOW...
HEY... FRANK... DO...
THANKS FOR THE HANKIE.
ANYTIME.

NO...
I...
DON'T CALL ME...
FRANK.
OH, I'M SORRY... I HEARD THE OTHER KIDS CALLING YOU THAT.
SOME GUY MADE IT UP. AS IN "FRANKENSTEIN."
BECAUSE OF MY FACE...
I'M SORRY... I DIDN'T KNOW!
SO WHAT IS YOUR NAME, THEN?
KYONOSUKE. YOU?
MY NAME'S AKIRA.
KYONOSUKE... WHAT'S YOUR FAVORITE MANGA?

I HAVEN'T MISSED A SINGLE EPISODE.
HA HA HA
TOTALLY! THE ANIME IS SO MUCH COOLER!
LEAVE ME ALONE.
THERE'S NO SMOKING HERE, KENTA. YOU'LL GET SUSPENDED.
DOOM
YO, CHECK OUT THE FREAKS, GUYS.
PFFFFFF

HA HA HA HA HA!!!
I BET YOU TWO LOSERS GET ALONG GREAT.
HAHA
CHILL, FRANK. I'M JUST HERE FOR A LITTLE DOUGH. YOU KNOW.
I DON'T HAVE ANY CASH ON ME. I SWEAR!
YOU STILL DON'T GET IT, DO YOU?!
POW

LEAVE HIM ALONE!
I'M NOT AFRAID OF YOU, KENTA.
BAM

CHAPTER 2

OW
OOOOO
DO WHATEVER YOU WANT.
I'M NOT AFRAID OF YOU.
JUST LET IT GO, DUDE.
LET'S BOUNCE. IT'S NOT WORTH IT.
OOOO...

YOU FREAKS GOT LUCKY THIS TIME.
NEXT TIME, I'LL DESTROY YOU.
HAS KENTA ALWAYS BEEN LIKE THAT?
YEP. HE LOVES TO BULLY OTHER STUDENTS.
SOME KIDS EVEN LEFT SCHOOL BECAUSE OF HIM.
S.RIDE
THANKS FOR YOUR HELP, BY THE WAY.
NAH, IT'S NOTHING!
USUALLY, NOBODY REALLY GIVES A CRAP ABOUT ME...
EXCEPT FOR MY PARENTS.

HEY...
...
...

HAVE YOU, UM...EVER HAD GRAPE KISS?
NO. NEVER TRIED IT.
...
SERIOUSLY? IT'S AWESOME. IT'S LIKE, MY FAVORITE DRINK.
YOU HAVE TO TRY IT.
ACTUALLY... NOW'S NOT THE BEST TIME. IT'S MOSTLY AVAILABLE IN THE SPRING AND SUMMER.
BUT IF I SEE ANY, I'LL GRAB YOU ONE.
UM... THANKS.

WELL... THIS IS ME.
COOL. SEE YOU LATER, THEN.
LATER.
HM...

POF
OK. BACKPACK, MONEY, THE LIST...
THAT'S EVERYTHING.
YOU SURE YOU'LL BE ALL RIGHT, SWEETIE?
IT'S JUST A FEW ERRANDS!
YEP.
DO YOU HAVE YOUR PHONE?

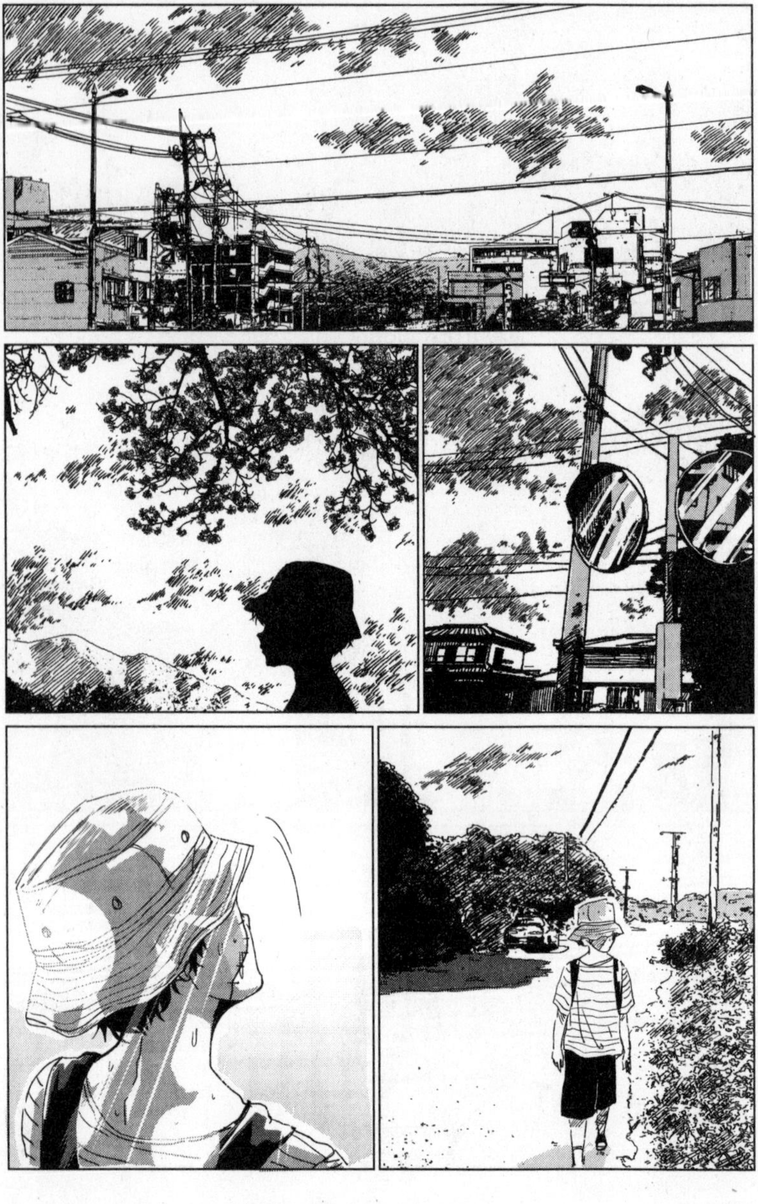

BROOOOOOOOO...

THAT'LL BE 760 YEN.
HERE YOU GO.
THANKS, HAVE A GREAT DAY.
WAIT A MINUTE...
YOU'RE DR. WATANABE'S SON, AREN'T YOU?
YES. WHY?
IT'S NICE TO SEE YOU OUT AND ABOUT.
KIRIM
KIRIM

IT FEELS NICE.
TAKE CARE OF YOURSELF, KID.
GOODBYE! THANKS!

MEOOW!
OH, WHAT A CUTE KITTY CAT!
PURR PURR
PURR PURR
PURR PURR
PURR PURR PURR
PURR PURR PURR
PURR

FLASH!
SMILE FOR THE CAMERA! HEH, HEH. AKIRA'S GONNA LOVE IT.
ALL RIGHT! LAST ONE!
FLASH
FLASH
FLASH
FLASH
FLASH
FLASH
FLASH
FLASH
FLASH
FLASH
WELL, WELL!
WHAT'S MY LITTLE ZOMBIE UP TO?
I HOPE YOU HAVE MONEY FOR ME TODAY.
97

YOU ALSO OWE ME CASH FROM LAST TIME. YOU DO REMEMBER, DON'T YOU?
OH...Y-YES, OF COURSE.
OK... B-BYE...

TCH!
HEY, BUTTHEAD!
IS THIS SOME
SORT OF JOKE?

BAM!
AAAH!

POF
?!
MAKOTO, HAND ME THE BAT.
I'M SICK OF YOUR STUPID FACE, LOSER!

AH...
AHH...
AHH...
AH...
FSH
VOOSH VOOSH
!!
HEY, MISTER! OVER HERE!
!
DASH

AARGH! THAT LITTLE PUNK!
NGH!
TAP
TAP
TAP
TAP
TAP
TAP
TAP
HUFF
HAAH HAAH
HUH
HAAH HAHH
HUFF HUFF
TAP
TAP
HE'S...
SMARTER ...
THAN HE LOOKS...
HUFF, HUFF, HUFF.
THAT LOSER THINKS HE CAN MOCK US...
BUT NEXT TIME, WE'LL CATCH HIM AND SMASH HIS FACE IN.

HUFF
HUFF HUFF
HUFF
AAH!
WHOA!

HAAH HAAH
HUFF HUFF HUFF
HAHH HAAH
HAAH HAHH
HUFF
I HAVE NO IDEA WHERE I AM...
HAAH HAHH
HUFF
HUFF

I'M TELLING YOU, MOM, I'M FINE.
GULP GULP GULP
...
HEY, THAT SOUNDS LIKE AKIRA!
DON'T WORRY ABOUT ME.

AKIRA!!!
AND... UP! HERE I GO!
AKIRA!
HUH?

I'M FINE!
PLEASE LEAVE
ME ALONE.

...
I...
...
JUST BEAT IT, OK!
I SAID I'M FINE! CAN'T YOU SEE I WANT TO BE ALONE?!

HERE. I FOUND SOME GRAPE KISS.
THEY GOT SOME IN TODAY.

BUT SINCE YOU'RE HERE...
I WAS GOING TO BRING IT TO SCHOOL FOR YOU.

THANKS.

CHAPTER 3

SCARS

HEY, KYONOSUKE.
HAVE YOU SEEN THE LATEST DOKI DOKI FILM, POWER LOVE?
LICK LICK
NOT YET, BUT I WAS THINKING OF GOING NEXT WEEK.
AWESOME.
DO YOU WANT TO COME WITH ME? MY TREAT.
SERIOUSLY? FOR REAL?
SURE!

I WILL NEVER LET YOU EXTINGUISH THE LIGHT IN MY HEART!
HER HEART... IT'S...
WOOOOOW
YOU ARE ABOUT TO DISCOVER THE TRUE POWER OF LOVE.

CINEMAZEMAX
I REALLY LOVED THE FILM TOO.
OH, MAN, THAT WAS SO *POWERFUL!*
WANNA GO GET SOME ICE CREAM?
SURE.

IT LOOKS DE-LI-CIOUS!
MY ICE CREAM...
SPLAT!
UH-OH, ICE CREAM DROP.
DIDN'T EVEN GET TO TASTE IT.
STAY RIGHT THERE, I'LL GET YOU ANOTHER ONE.
WOOOOOAH
IT'S HUGE!
THANKS, KYONOSUKE!
SURE THING...
NO WORRIES. THIRD TIME'S THE CHARM!
DOUBLE DROP
OH, MAAAAN.—
THANKS, KYONOSUKE... YOU'RE REALLY SWEET.
SURE THING.

STAR STAR

YOU REALLY EXPECT ME TO BELIEVE YOU DON'T HAVE ANY MONEY ON YOU, KENTA?!
ARE YOU TAKING THE PISS OUTTA ME?!
TELL ME THE TRUTH!
YOU ALREADY BLEW IT ALL, DIDN'T YOU?!
NO, I DIDN'T, DAD! I SWEAR!
I'LL GO BACK AND FIND SOME MONEY RIGHT NOW...
BUT PLEASE, STOP HITTING ME.
FINE.
BUT MAKE IT QUICK!

I GOT YOU A CHOCOLATE ONE, YOUR FAVORITE!
THANKS, SON.
IT'S ALL OVER YOUR FACE!
HA HA HA!

WHERE'S YOUR SON?
NO IDEA.
BUT HE WON'T HAVE THE GUTS TO SHOW UP EMPTY-HANDED THIS TIME.

BYE.
I'LL SEE YOU LATER.
CALL ME.
HEY! THERE'S A KID OUT HERE!
HE'S SLEEPING!
WAKE HIM UP WITH THE GARDEN HOSE!!!
I BET IT'S KENTA!
YOU HANDLE IT, I GOTTA GO!

OH.
FLAP
FLAP
FLAP...

BOIL
BOIL
BOIL...
SCRAPE
SCRAPE
DAD...
IT'S READY!

WE'RE OUTTA BEER.
GO FIND SOME MONEY AND BUY SOME.
NOW!
OK.

SMILE, BE HAPPY ♪
TAP

ROLL
ROLL
ROLL
AAAH
GRAB!
EMPTY YOUR POCKETS, MORON!
BAM
AAAH!!
O- OK!
PLEASE D-DON'T HURT ME...

UGHH...
BDAAAAM

WOW, YOU REALLY WENT AT HIM.
HE'S KNOCKED OUT.
YOU THINK WE KILLED HIM?
DON'T TALK LIKE THAT.
BESIDES, *HE'S* THE ONE WHO ATTACKED US. THIS IS NOT OUR PROBLEM.
STILL, WE SHOULD GET THE HELL OUTTA HERE.
FOR SURE.

HEY, KID.
HE'S UNRESPON-SIVE.
CALL AN AMBULANCE.
OK.

WHAT HAPPENED TO HIM?
HE MUST HAVE BEEN ATTACKED. THE POLICE WILL HANDLE IT.
FSH!!
?!
YOU THERE! ARE YOU ALL RIGHT?!
WHAT HAPPENED?!
HEY!
TAP TAP TAP

I...
WHERE'S MY BEER?!
...
HEY! DO YOU HAVE MY FREAKING BEER OR NOT?!
IT'S JUST... THERE WAS A PROBLEM AND—

YOU'RE A USELESS PIECE OF SHIT.
I KNOW ...
YOU KNOW WHAT, KENTA?
WHAT...?

USELESS PIECE OF SHIT!
I'M KICKING YOUR ASS OUT!!
AGGH
GHHK
FSHH
BAAAM!
LEAVE ME ALONE!!!
FSH

HUFF
HUFF
HUFF
GRAB
DOOM

BAAM
WHO THE HELL DO YOU THINK YOU ARE, YOU RUNT?
D-DAD...
I'M SORRY... FORGIVE ME, PLEASE. I BEG YOU.

AAAH! DAD, STOP!
BIM BAM BOOM
BIM BAM BOOM
STOP IT!
DAAAD!
STOP, YOU'RE HURTING ME!
SHUT UP!
YOU LITTLE PIECE OF SHIT!
PLEASE...
I'M SORRY...
FORGIVE...
ME...
HUFF
HUFF
HUFF
HUFF
HUFF
HUFF

QUIT BAWLING LIKE A LITTLE BITCH.
KYONOSUKE, I THINK WE SHOULD LEAVE...
DON'T BOTHER COMING HOME TOMORROW WITHOUT MONEY.
NO FREELOADERS IN MY HOUSE.
SLAM
SNIFF
ANTA
SNIFF
SNIFF
SNIFF

KYONOSUKE! WAIT! DON'T DO IT!
...
WHOOOOSH

TCH...
HEY! WHAT IS YOUR PROBLEM, DUDE?!
WHAT THE HELL DO YOU WANT, FREAK?
HAVE YOU SEEN YOUR FACE?!
YOU'RE ONE TO TALK!
HMPF. JERK!
COME ON, KYONOSUKE. LET'S GO.

HERE. TO RINSE OFF.
...

THANKS.
NOW BEAT IT,
BOTH OF YOU!
YOU SHOULD
REPORT HIM.

WHAT THE HELL ARE YOU TALKING ABOUT, ZOMBIE?
COME ON, KYONOSUKE! WE REALLY HAVE TO GO!
TAKE CARE OF YOURSELF.

CHAPTER 4

SCARS

TAP
TAP
TAP
OH...
KYONOSUKE!
HI, AKIRA. I WAS ABOUT TO GO GET LUNCH.

NO, I... I MADE SOMETHING FOR YOU.
WE CAN EAT TOGETHER, IF YOU WANT.
IS SOMETHING WRONG?
YOU'RE SO SWEET.
YOU SHOULDN'T HAVE.
OH, IT'S NOTHING, REALLY.
FOR ME?

MUSTA BEEN ONE HELL OF A FIGHT.
NEXT TIME, CALL US.
YEAH! EVER SINCE AKIRA SAVED HIS ASS, THEY'VE BEEN INSEPARABLE.
HAVE YOU NOTICED? ZOMBIE AND AKIRA ARE JOINED AT THE HIP NOW.
THERE ARE EVEN PICS GOING AROUND.
HEY, GUYS.
GUESS THOSE DEGENERATES WERE MADE FOR EACH OTHER.
HA HA HA

I NEED TO TELL HER...
BUT I DON'T KNOW HOW.
I'VE NEVER DONE THIS BEFORE...
WHAT IF SHE JUST WANTS TO BE FRIENDS...?
OK, HERE I GO... I'M DOING IT!
AKIRA, I...
?

WHAT'S WRONG?
YOU DON'T WANT TO TRY THE DISH I MADE FOR YOU?
...
WHY AM I FREEZING UP LIKE THIS?!
I HAVE TO TELL HER...
I CAN'T SEEM TO GET THE WORDS OUT...
IS IT FEAR?
MY EMOTIONS?
SNAP OUT OF IT, DUDE!

AKIRA, I-I REALLY, REALLY LIKE YOU!

KYO...I...
SERIOUSLY?
ARE YOU FREAKING SERIOUS, FRANKENSTEIN?!
THE WEIRDO WITH A THING FOR WEIRDOS! HA HA HA!
ARE YOU REALLY CRUSHING ON AKIRA?

WHAT IF I AM? WHAT BUSINESS IS IT OF YOURS?
JUST STAY AWAY FROM HER!
WHOA! CHILLAX, FRANK, IT'S COOL.
WE DON'T GIVE A RAT'S ASS IF YOU LIKE BOYS.
WHAT WAS THAT, AKIRA? YOU HAVEN'T SHOWN HIM YOUR LITTLE BALLS, YET?
HAHAHAHA
HAHAHAHA

HA HA HA HA
STOP IT, DUDE! I'M GONNA PISS MY PANTS!
HA HA HA HA HA HA
AKIRA...
I... I...
AKIRA, WAIT!
TAP TAP TAP TAP TAP TAP

YOU'D BETTER RUN!
WSH
HE'S GETTING AWAY!
DAAM
UGH
DUDE! WHAT THE HELL?!
WHY DID YOU HIT JUNYA?!

SNIFF
SNIFF
...
RUSTLE
...
WHAT ARE YOU DOING HERE?

YOU WANT AN APOLOGY, IS THAT IT?
I'M SORRY... I KNOW WHAT I DID TO YOU WAS AWFUL.
FORGIVE ME...
PLEASE FORGIVE ME.
AKIRA...

I JUST WANT YOU TO KNOW...
THAT IT DOESN'T CHANGE MY FEELINGS FOR YOU.

TAC TAC
TAC
TAC
TAC
TAC...
CLIK
CLIK
CLIK
CLIK
CLIK
I NEVER THOUGHT JUNYA WOULD SPILL THE BEANS ABOUT THOSE TWO.
TAC
TAC
TAC
Stargram
yukoo_97
yukoo_97
Losers hooking up.
Check out the freaks.
#weirdos
HA HA. TOO CUTE.

Comments
Unoi: So it was true?
Hide: o
Gokuu: I knew it! They've been inseparable!
Panooo: What?? Akira has a crush?
+9
yukoo_97
Losers hooking up.
Check out the freaks.
TAC
TAC
TAC
SOTAAAPUNK
Junya97: Not only is zombie head butt ugly, but he's a freaking fag too! Hahahaha
TAC
GIF
Q W E R T Y U I O P
TAC
S D F G L Ñ
TAC

MOM, I'M LEAVING NOW.
HAVE A GREAT DAY, SWEETIE.
SHE MUST STILL BE SLEEPING...
8:01
last seen today at 13:25
13:24
Hey Akira :) Just walked out the door. Waiting for you.
8:00
Type a message

AKIRA, OPEN THIS DOOR!
BOM
BOM
BOM
BOM
BOM
WHAT THE HELL IS GOING ON?!
BOM
BOM
BOM
BOM
BOM
BOM
AKIRAAAA!
BOM
BOM
BOM
BOM
BOM
OPEN UP, DAMMIT!
BOM
BOM
BOM
BOM

!
yukoo_97
follow
89
62
20
yukoo_97
Losers hooking up.
Check out the freaks.
#weirdos

AKIRA!

BRR...
BRR...
BRR...
BRR...
BR...
BRRR...
BRRR...
akira
AKIRA!
HELLO?
THIS IS AKIRA'S DAD SPEAKING.
ARE YOU THE PERVERT HANGING OUT WITH MY SON?!
...

NOW YOU LISTEN TO ME, YOU LITTLE PUNK.
IF I EVER CATCH YOU HOVERING AROUND HIM AGAIN...
I'LL CALL THE POLICE AND HAVE YOU ARRESTED FOR HARASSMENT!
BIP

HEY!

FRANKENSTEIN! YOU'RE NOT IN CLASS. WHAT'S GOING ON, LOSER?
WHAT'S WRONG WITH YOUR EYES? WERE YOU CRYING? HA HA HA!
FRR
FRR
FRR
DID YOU AND AKIRA HAVE A FIGHT? YOU WERE MAKING OUT JUST YESTERDAY!

N-NO.
WHAT? I CAN'T HEAR YOU!
NO... NO, I...
BLAAAM

OUCH... THAT LOOKED LIKE IT HURT.
YOU'RE JUST A BIG MEANIE, JUNYA.
HEY, I HURT MY KNEE! YOU'RE THE MEANIE!
NGH...
GNN
HNGH
SORRY ABOUT THAT, ZOMBIE.
NEXT TIME, I'LL GO EASIER ON YOU...OR NOT! WE'LL JUST HAVE TO SEE.
HA HA HA HA

CHAPTER 5

SCARS

BRR! BRR!
Mom
BRR! BRR! BRR!
BRR! BRR! BRR!

HELLO...
KYONOSUKE! YOU PICKED UP! FINALLY!
ARE YOU ALL RIGHT?
DID SOMETHING HAPPEN?
...
KYONOSUKE!
ANSWER ME! WHAT'S GOING ON?!

TALK TO ME, SWEETIE!!!
I'M FINE...
I'M... COMING HOME.
WHAT DID HE SAY?
IS HE ALL RIGHT?
HE'S FINE. HE'S ON HIS WAY HOME.
SNIFF

SHOULDN'T HE BE HERE ALREADY?
YOU ONLY JUST SPOKE TO HIM ON THE PHONE.
I'M BACK...
SWEET-HEART!
WHAT HAPPENED TO YOU?!

COME ON, KIDDO.
...
YOU CAN TRUST US.
NO MATTER WHAT...
WE'RE HERE TO SUPPORT YOU.

I-I'M...
IN LOVE.
SO *THAT'S* WHAT THIS IS...
LISTEN, KIDDO, I KNOW HOW FRAGILE YOU ARE...
BUT THE WORLD WON'T ALWAYS BE CRUEL TO YOU.

I'M SURE YOU'LL FIND THE RIGHT GIRL ONE DAY!
YOU HAVE TO KEEP MOVING FORWARD!
THANKS, DAD. IT FEELS GOOD TO HEAR YOU SAY THAT.
I REALLY LOVE HER. EVEN THOUGH SHE'S A BOY...
...
SHE SEES HERSELF...AS A GIRL.

SLAP

I NEVER WANT TO HEAR ABOUT THIS AGAIN!
WE'VE NEVER HAD THIS SORT OF SCANDAL IN OUR FAMILY!
YOU'RE GOING TO PROMISE ME IT WON'T HAPPEN AGAIN, DO YOU HEAR?!
SWEET-HEART...
DO YOU SEE WHAT YOU'RE PUTTING YOUR POOR FATHER THROUGH? TELL HIM IT'S OVER.

IT'S OVER, DAD, I PROMISE.
YOU'LL NEVER HEAR ABOUT THIS RELATIONSHIP EVER AGAIN.
SNIFF
SNIFF
BUAAH
HAHH...
BRRR! BRRR!

Chats 1
Unknown number
New message
Mom
Yes, sweetie, that's fine
Akira
Akira, answer me...
Dad
They only have Book 3, kiddo.
WHO COULD THAT BE?
OH, MAYBE IT'S...!
Chats
Unknown number
Kyonosuke, it's Akira
I'm running away tonight...
Wanna come with me? Please answer ASAP!
Unknown number
New me
TAP

WHOA!
FRSSH
SAVINGS
SAVINGS

THIS IS NUTS...DID I REALLY JUST RUN AWAY?
MOM... DAD...
MY WHOLE LIFE...

NO.
THERE'S NO NEED TO BE AFRAID!
I'VE GOT AKIRA!
AKIRA IS MY LIFE FROM NOW ON!

KYONOSUKE!
AKIRA!

WHAT...
WHAT HAPPENED?
...
IT'S...
MY DAD.

DON'T CRY.
I PROMISE EVERYTHING WILL BE OK NOW.
SNIFF
SNIFF

WE'RE LEAVING.
THE VIOLENCE, OUR PARENTS...
THAT'S ALL OVER.
FROM NOW ON, IT'S JUST THE TWO OF US.
FAR AWAY FROM THIS NIGHTMARE.
YES...

AKIRA...
KYO...
PROMISE ME!
PROMISE YOU'LL NEVER EVER LEAVE ME!
I PROMISE.
I'LL NEVER LEAVE YOU.

TATAM
TATAM
TATAM
COME ON, LIGHT UP!
CRR
CRR

WHAT IS IT?
HEY!
YOU GUYS GOT A LIGHT?
UH, NO... SORRY.
UGH...
MY LIGHTER JUST DIED.

WHAT ARE YOU TWO DOING HERE?
OH MY GOD! YOU'RE RUNNING AWAY!
I...
WE...
IT'S JUST...
RELAX, GUYS.
I WON'T TELL ANYONE.
!

REALLY?! THANKS!
NO BIGGIE.
DON'T WORRY.
THANKS... KENTA.
I SAID IT'S NO BIG DEAL.
WHAT ARE YOU DOING HERE, KENTA?
NOTHING... I WAS BORED AT SCHOOL.
I FELT LIKE GETTING OUT FOR A BIT, SO I TOOK OFF.

TATAM
TATAM
TATAM
TATAM
KENTA?
?
SEE... SEE YOU?

10
TATAM
TATAM
TATAM

HEY, KID! HAVE YOU SEEN THIS BOY?!
HMMM...
YEAH, THAT'S KYONOSUKE. I JUST SAW HIM.
HE WAS HEADED FOR THE AIRPORT IN A TAXI.
I THINK HE SAID HE WAS GOING TO...
CHINA. YEAH, THAT'S IT. CHINA.
CHINA?!

CHAPTER 6

SCARS

KYONOSUKE...
CAN YOU HEAR ME?
WAKE UP!
KAORI?
YOUR MOM SAID TO WAKE YOU UP!
COME ON, GET UP! THERE'S LOTS OF FRESH SNOW!
LOOK!
I BROUGHT MY SLED!

IT'S AWESOME, RIGHT?!
IT'S GONNA BE SO MUCH FUN!
YOU WANNA GO FIRST?
OH! I... IT'S JUST THAT...
I'M A LITTLE NERVOUS.
...

DON'T WORRY, KYONOSUKE.
WE CAN GO DOWN TOGETHER.
NO NEED TO BE AFRAID.
I'LL PROTECT YOU!
OK, LET'S GO!

KYONOSUKE!
CHECK IT OUT!
I CAN SKIP STONES!
PLAP
PLAP
PLAP
THERE!
WOW, THIS IS SO COOL!
TRY IT, COME ON!
SPLASH!
DON'T WORRY.
I'LL TEACH YOU.

AAH...
KAORI...
YOU'RE A PATHETIC WIMP, KYONOSUKE!
ASKING A *GIRL* FOR HELP!
HEY! LEAVE HIM ALONE!
YOU *DON'T WANT* TO SEE ME GET ANGRY.
HEY! STOP PUSHING ME!
LETTING A *GIRL* PROTECT YOU!
YOU LITTLE FAGGOT!
THEY'RE GONE.
LET'S GET YOU PATCHED UP.

I'M READY.
WELL?
WHAT DO YOU THINK?
YOU LOOK...
VERY PRETTY.
KYONOSUKE?
WHAT'S WRONG?

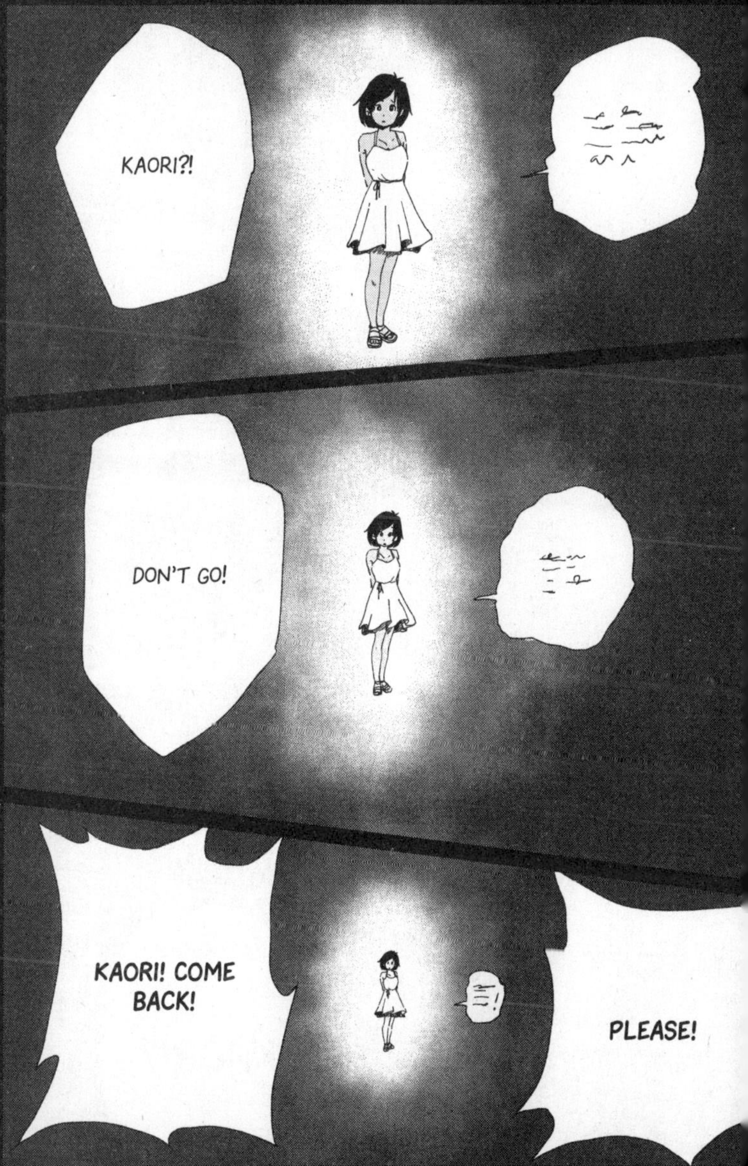
KAORI?!
DON'T GO!
KAORI! COME BACK!
PLEASE!

WHAT HAPPENED?
KAORI?
NO! NO NO NO NO...

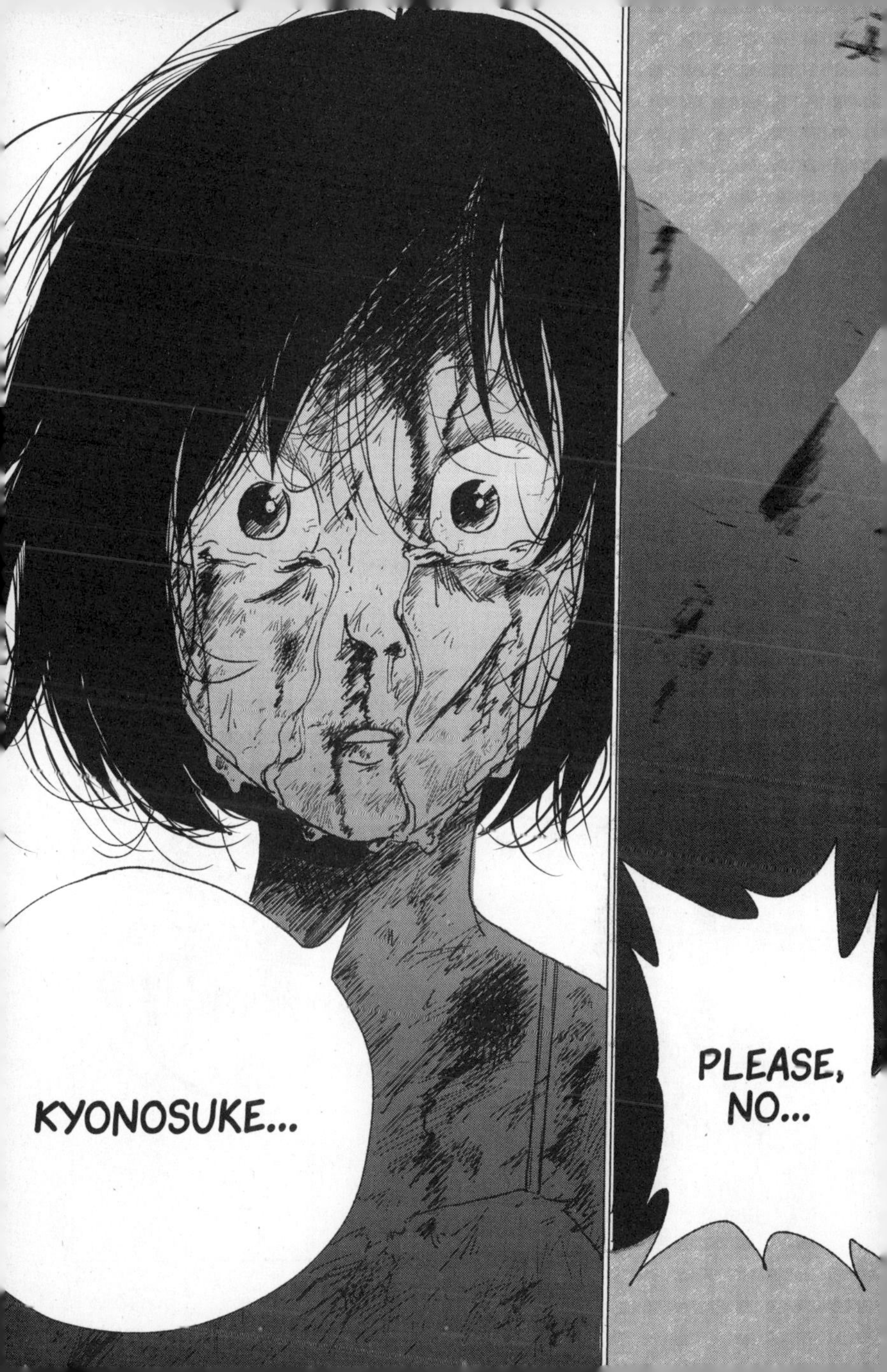
PLEASE, NO...
KYONOSUKE...

AAAH!
HAHH
HAA...
ARE YOU ALL RIGHT?
WHAT WERE YOU DREAMING ABOUT?
I... UM...
I CAN'T REMEMBER.
THIS IS OUR STATION. TIME TO GET OFF.
OH, RIGHT.

HAVE YOU BEEN HERE BEFORE?
NO.
OK, SO... NOW WHAT DO WE DO?
HMMM...
WE NEED A PLACE TO SLEEP. WHICH WILL COST MONEY.
SO FIRST, WE NEED TO FIND WORK.
SORNY
HIS NAME IS KYONOSUKE.
HE'S 15.
HE HAS A VERY DISTINCTIVE SCAR.

WHAT'S WRONG?
LOOK!
THEY RAN AWAY TOGETHER...
SORNY
IF YOU SEE THEM, PLEASE CALL THE POLICE IMMEDIATELY.
?
THAT ALERT WILL HAVE THEM LOOKING FOR US IN EVERY HOTEL IN THE AREA!
WHAT DO WE DO?
COME ON!
I HAVE AN IDEA!

WE'LL PUT THESE WIGS ON.
I'M BACK!
THIS SHOULD THROW THEM OFF OUR TRAIL.
HOW... HOW DO I LOOK?

HELLO, SIR!
SORRY TO BOTHER YOU. WE'RE HERE ABOUT THE AD.
HOW OLD ARE YOU?
UM... WE'RE IN HIGH SCHOOL.
NOPE!
COME BACK WHEN YOU'RE IN COLLEGE!
IT'LL BE THE SAME EVERYWHERE.

NOBODY WILL WANT TO HIRE US.
HE'S RIGHT.
MAYBE... MAYBE RUNNING AWAY FROM HOME WAS A BAD IDEA.
DON'T SAY THAT!
YOU CAN'T JUST GIVE UP AS SOON AS IT GETS TOUGH!
...
I...

I'M REALLY SCARED.
WHERE WILL WE SLEEP?
WHAT ARE WE GOING TO DO?
OH, AKIRA...
AS LONG AS WE'RE TOGETHER...
WE CAN OVERCOME ANYTHING.
OK.
AKIRA LOOKS EXHAUSTED.
I HAVE TO PROTECT HER.
OH, CRAP...
SHE'S BURNING UP!

HAAH
HUFF
HUFF
HAAH
HUFF
THIS HOUSE LOOKS ABANDONED!
KYO... KYONOSUKE?
STAY HERE. I'LL BE RIGHT BACK.
HEY, YOU!
WHAT THE HELL ARE YOU DOING HERE?!

AH! I...I'M SORRY, SIR!
BOOM
AAAAAAAAAAAAH!!!
I'LL KILL YOU!
SO WHAT?!
WELL, PUNKS?
WHERE'D YOU COME FROM?!
BAM!
CAN'T YOU SEE THEY'RE JUST KIDS, YOU IDIOT?
WE NEED HELP...

I WON'T LET ANYONE TRESPASS ON MY PRIVATE PROPERTY.
BEAT IT. BOTH YOU AND YOUR MESSED-UP FRIEND.
SHUT UP! WE CAN'T JUST LEAVE THEM LIKE THIS!!
POW!
AKIRA ...
NHH!
I FOUND SOME MEDICINE.
THANKS!

ZZZ...
GIVE HER THE PILLS AND THEN LET HER REST.
OK.
THANKS FOR EVERYTHING, MA'AM. WE HAD NOWHERE ELSE TO GO...
YEAH, YEAH. NOW TELL ME...
WHY DID YOU TWO KIDS RUN AWAY?
OK... I'LL TELL YOU.

DON'T WORRY.
I'LL LET THEM STAY HERE.
YIKES. THAT'S REALLY HARSH, DUDE.
BUT IT'S NOT FREE! IN EXCHANGE, YOU WILL BOTH WORK IN MY RESTAURANT.
CALL ME MRS. AIKO.
REALLY?!
OH THANKS, MA'AM!
YOU HAVE SUCH A BIG HEART.
HMPF.
OK, MRS. AIKO!
WE'LL DO WHATEVER YOU ASK!

居酒屋六
I'M STILL NOT USED TO THE ORANGE DYE JOB YOU GAVE ME.
IT SUITS YOU.
BREAK'S OVER! TIME TO CLOSE UP!
YES, MRS. AIKO!

GREETINGS, ALL!
HI, KOICHI!
HI!
LALALA LALALA!
LALALA LA LALALA!
WHAT ARE YOU KIDS UP TO TOMORROW?
WF. COULD GO TO THE BEACH AND WATCH THE FIREWORKS.
WHAT DO YOU THINK, KYONOSUKE?
SURE, SOUNDS LIKE FUN!
IT'S SETTLED, THEN!
IT'S GONNA BE AN AWESOME DAY!

AKIII-RAAAA...
ARE YOU READY YET?
YES...
I AM NOW.
HURRY UP, KIDS!
SHALL WE?
WHOA... YES!

居酒屋六
IT'S ABOUT TIME!
SORRY!
COME ON, LET'S GO!

OUCH! HOT, HOT, HOT!
I FEEL SO... HAPPY.
PSH! PSH!
DON'T SPIT IT OUT, YOU INGRATE!
HA HA HA
FIZZ FIZZ FIZZ
THANKS FOR COMING WITH ME.
I DON'T KNOW WHAT I WOULD'VE DONE, ALL BY MYSELF...

WOULD YOU DO THAT, MY LOVE? RUN AWAY WITH ME?
HMM...IF I STILL LOVED YOU, SURE.
SUCH ADORABLE KIDS...
FACING HARDSHIP TOGETHER.
BOOM
BOOM
BAAM
BAAM
BOOM
PTCHOOO
IT STARTED!
OH...IT'S STARTING!

AWWW... THAT'S SO SWEET...

HEY, KIDS! COME IN AND JOIN THE PARTY!
MY TREAT!
THANKS! WE'LL BE RIGHT UP!
I CAN'T BELIEVE HOW NICE HE IS. TO THINK HE ALMOST KILLED US!
THAT WAS NOT NICE!
THIS ICE CREAM IS SOOO GOOD!

ONE, TWO...
CLIK!
IT FELT TRULY MAGICAL.
OUR PROBLEMS DIDN'T EXIST ANYMORE.

EVERYTHING WAS PERFECT.
WE WANTED THAT MOMENT TO LAST FOREVER.
BUT NOTHING...
LASTS FOREVER.

TO BE CONTINUED

SCARS

BONUS

BRANDON ARIAS

I LOVE SPIDER-MAN.
I ♡ SPIDER MAN
I'M A BIG FAN OF CLARENCE.
I LOVE WATCHING THE SUN GO DOWN.
I LOVE SUNSETS.

SKETCHBOOK

KYONOSUKE, 15

What is the story you wanted to tell with *Scars*?
I wanted a story that was brutal, and nothing is more brutal than reality.

What part of the first book did you most enjoy drawing?
The touching scenes with deep feelings, like Kenta's first chapter, which I found very moving. I hope readers respond to it the same way. I was very moved as I wrote it.

How and when did you learn to draw manga?

I learned to draw by doing research on the Internet when I was 21. At that time, I was part of a punk band that wasn't doing too great. I started drawing in my spare time. I bought a tablet, and at first I would just draw with my finger, but then I eventually bought a stylus, too, and I started taking it more seriously.

Who are your favorite manga authors, the ones who have most influenced you?

My biggest inspiration was Asano Inio. The first seinen manga I read was one of his. I love his melancholy and his sadness. Then I discovered the works of Oshimi Shuzo and Shinzo Keigo. They also had a big impact on me. I became obsessed. I was fascinated by the mundane nature of their works—that and the conflict, which, every single time, grows more and more intense, and keeps us guessing as to how it will be resolved.

BRANDON ARIAS was born in Santiago, Chile, in 1997.

One of Brandon's first passions was punk music, soon to be followed by manga, which he discovered via authors like Asano Inio, Oshimi Shuzo, and Shinzo Keigo. It wasn't long before he was trying his hand at short stories that he published independently on different digital platforms. Like his masters, he explores the complexities of human relationships, often between adolescents, through portraits of everyday life colored by a highly sensitive point of view.

Scars is his first professional series as a full-fledged artist.

SCARS

SCARS VOLUME 1
BY BRANDON ARIAS

Designer: Shawn Dahl
Editor: Kristi Iwashiro
Editorial Assistant: Kai Obinata
Managing Editor: Marie Oishi
Production Manager: Sarah Masterson Hally

Adapted into English by Nube Consulting
Translation: Montana Kane
Letterer: Thomas

Original layout: Léa Ellinckhuÿsen
Original cover design: Ayumi KANEKO

Library of Congress Control Number 2024936150
ISBN: 978-1-4197-7835-3
eISBN: 979-8-88707-490-0

First published in France in 2024 by Vega-Dupuis, an imprint of Editions Dupuis.

English language translation rights arranged with Média-Participations through Mediatoon, Paris.

Printed and bound in Italy
10 9 8 7 6 5 4 3 2 1

PEFC
PEFC/18-31-280

ABRAMS The Art of Books
195 Broadway, New York, NY 10007
abramsbooks.com

THIS MANGA HAS BEEN PUBLISHED IN ITS ORIGINAL READING DIRECTION, FROM RIGHT TO LEFT

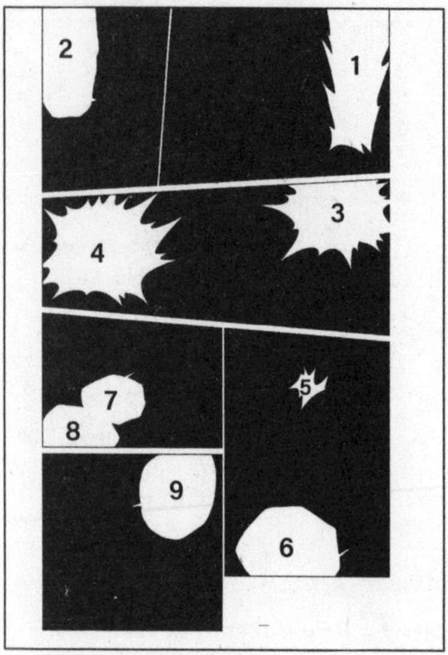

THIS IS THE END

SCARS

kana